For my girls, I love you big!

— K.G.

For Junie and Jalen.
You are Truly fierce and fabulous!

— A.R.

Library of Congress Cataloging-in-Publication Data • Names: Greenawalt, Kelly, author. | Rauscher, Amariah, illustrator. • Title: Princess Truly in I am Truly / by Kelly Greenawalt ; illustrated by Amariah Rauscher. • Other titles: I am Truly • Description: First edition. | New York : Orchard Books, an imprint of Scholastic Inc., 2017. | Summary: "Princess Truly's rhyming adventures are a celebration of individuality, girl power, diversity, and dreaming big!"—Provided by publisher. • Identifiers: LCCN 2016050195 (print) | LCCN 2017004676 (ebook) | ISBN 9781338167207 (hardcover : alk. paper) ISBN 9781338184907 • Subjects: | CYAC: Stories in rhyme. | Princesses—Fiction. • Classification: LCC PZ8.3.G7495 Pr 2017 (print) | LCC PZ8.3.G7495 (ebook) | DDC [E]—dc23 • LC record available at https://lccn.loc.gov/2016050195

10 9 8 7 6 5 4 3 2 1   17 18 19 20 21 • Printed in the U.S.A. 88 • First edition, August 2017

Book design by Patti Ann Harris

PRINCESS TRULY in
I Am TRULY

by
Kelly Greenawalt

illustrated by
Amariah Rauscher

Orchard Books
An Imprint of Scholastic Inc.
New York

I am Truly.

I like frogs
and the color blue.
I can climb trees
and be a rock star, too.

I can run fast
and build tall towers.

I am a superhero
with magical powers.

I am smart,

I am studious,

I am a high achiever.

I am strong,
I am skillful,
I am a born leader.

I can sail the seas
on a little boat.
I can eat every bite
of a root beer float.

I can tie
my own shoes.
I can find treasure
with clues.

I am clever,
I am curious,
I am an engineer.

I am confident,
I am courageous,
I am a volunteer.

I can fly to the moon

and dance on the stars.

I can tame wild lions
and race fast cars.

I can swim like a fish.
I can shoot and swish.

I am funny,
I am flexible,
I am an entertainer.

I am focused,
I am fierce,
I am a dinosaur trainer.

I can grow
purple grapes.
I can create
amazing shapes.

I can feed
hungry bunnies
crunchy carrots.

I can learn
Japanese
and teach it
to parrots.

I am Truly, watch me soar.
I am small but mighty,
hear me R RRRROOC

I can do anything
I set my mind to do.

Do you know that you
can do all these things, too?

You are Truly Fabulous!

Dear Readers:

We created Princess Truly for our daughters. We wanted them to see a strong, smart, problem-solving, confident young girl with beautiful curls who could do anything she set her mind to! We hope these books inspire readers everywhere to reach for the stars, dream big, and stay TRUE to who they are.

Kelly

Amariah

Kelly and her daughters,
Calista and Kaia

Amariah with her daughters,
Jalen and Junie